Truly Winnie

Truly Winnie

by Jennifer Richard Jacobson
Illustrated by Alissa Imre Geis

Houghton Mifflin Company
Boston

The author wishes to thank Toni Buzzeo, Jacqueline Davies, Mary Atkinson, Dana Walrath, and Holly Jacobson—first readers extraordinaire, and Franny Billingsley for coining "single bingle." Many thanks, too, to Ann Rider, who has believed in Winnie from the start.

www.houghtonmifflinbooks.com

The text of this book is set in Utopia.
The illustrations are graphite and caran d'ache crayon on bristol.

Library of Congress Cataloging-in-Publication Data is on file.

ISBN 0-618-28008-1

Manufactured in the United States of America
QUM 10 9 8 7 6 5 4 3 2

For my famous mother, for teaching me what is real.
—J.R.J.

For Whitney.
—A.I.G.

Chapter 1

"It says here that I should have *six* pairs of shorts," said Winnie. "But I only have five."

"Oh," said Mr. Fletcher. "It's too late to buy another pair now. Do you have any pants that are too small?"

Winnie hunted through her drawers. She pulled out a pair of jeans that she had grown too tall for. "How about these?"

"Perfect!" said Winnie's father. He held the pants up to Winnie, then pulled out scissors from Winnie's desk drawer and cut the bottom of the legs off. "There!" he said. "Six pairs of shorts."

Winnie held the shorts up. One leg was a little longer than the other. She waited for her dad to leave the room and then placed the shorts at the very bottom of the pile.

Winnie took another look at the list the camp had sent. "I think that's all I need," she called out.

"Not so fast," said her father. He returned with a roll of duct tape. "Here's one more thing no camper should be without."

Winnie looked at her overflowing trunk. Would other girls bring "duck tape," as she and her father called it? She doubted it. But Winnie was used to being different from other girls. "Thanks, Dad," she said, and stuffed the tape into a corner.

"Hey there!" said a voice behind Winnie.

Winnie knew without even turning that it was

Vanessa. Winnie and Vanessa lived in the same house on Clementine Street. Winnie and Mr. Fletcher lived on the first floor. Vanessa and her family lived on the second and third floors.

"Ready to go?" asked Vanessa.

"Now I am," said Winnie, slamming her trunk shut.

"Okay then, let's go!" said Mr. Fletcher. He lifted the trunk onto his shoulder and began the walk to the school parking lot, where a bus was waiting for them.

"Where is your stuff?" Winnie asked Vanessa.

"My parents carried it down earlier. Isn't this exciting?" said Vanessa. She was doing crazy pirouettes with her stuffed monkey, Bo Bo, as they walked along the sidewalk.

Winnie tried to smile, but she ended up stretching her mouth into a toothy line instead. She knew that she probably looked more nervous than excited.

"*I said boom!*" called a familiar voice.

Winnie and Vanessa turned to see their friend Zoe coming up behind them. She was carrying a sleeping bag in one hand and a duffel bag in the other. Zoe lived in the same neighborhood as Winnie and Vanessa, and the three girls had been best friends since kindergarten. Now they were going to overnight camp for the first time, and for two whole weeks!

Zoe ran up to Winnie and Vanessa and they chanted loudly:

"I said boom!
I said boom chicka-boom!
I said booma-chicka-rocka-chicka-
rocka-chicka-boom!
Uh huh!
Oh yeah!
One more time..."

After the trunks and bags were loaded onto the bus, it was time to say goodbye.

Mr. Fletcher crouched down to look Winnie in the eye. "You're going to have a great time, Win. I just know you are. You're a natural-born camper."

Suddenly Winnie felt her eyes burn. What if she and her friends were in different tents? What if the kids liked Vanessa (who was crazy and fun) and Zoe (who was smart and easygoing), but didn't like her (who was plain and boring)? What if her dad did all their favorite things, like eating pad thai with chopsticks and visiting the meerkats at the zoo, while she was gone?

"But what if it's not fun?" asked Winnie.

"It will be, you'll see," said Mr. Fletcher.

"Are you sure you can't come on Visitors' Day?"

"How I wish I could," said Mr. Fletcher, taking Winnie's hands in his.

Winnie nodded. She knew that her dad taught a class on Saturdays.

"But Vanessa's and Zoe's parents are coming and they'll treat you like one of their own," said Mr. Fletcher.

It was true. But it was hardly the same as having your *own* parent there.

"All aboard!" shouted the bus driver.

Winnie hugged her dad and followed Vanessa and Zoe onto the bus. The three girls squished into one seat.

"Only two to a seat," the driver called back.

It was Winnie's turn to be "odd girl out." The girls always kept track. She climbed over Zoe and slid into the empty seat in front of her best friends.

Zoe and Vanessa began talking about all of the things that they would do at camp. Winnie looked out at her father, standing alone among the other moms and dads, and thought how she didn't feel at all like a natural-born camper.

Chapter 2

A counselor named Spunky brought the girls to their camping area, called Treetops. Six tents on wooden platforms surrounded a fire circle in the woods. On the front of each tent was a list of names.

The girls ran from tent to tent, trying to find theirs.

"Here I am!" shouted Vanessa.

"Me, too," said Zoe, pointing to her name, directly under Vanessa's.

Winnie stared at the list, hoping that she had simply missed her name at first glance, but it was not there. The first thing she'd feared had happened.

"Oh, Winnie. We'll beg the counselors to switch you," said Vanessa.

"First let's find your tent," said Zoe. "Maybe it's close."

They checked the list on the tent to the left of Zoe and Vanessa's. Winnie's name wasn't there. They checked the list to the right of Zoe and Vanessa's. There it was: *Winifred Fletcher*.

"Wow! Look at this!" said Zoe, peeking behind the tent flap.

Inside Winnie's tent were four beds and four rickety crates to be used as shelves. One of the beds was already made with a bright blue sleeping bag that had pictures of leaping horses all over it. The pillow was puffy and in the shape of a star. Lying on the pillow was a stuffed horse. On the posts that held mosquito netting hung bright yellow stars that Winnie knew would glow in the dark.

The girls came closer to the mysterious belongings.

"Look what she brought," said Winnie.

Next to the bed, on the crate, was a blue ribbon with the words FIRST PRIZE and two pictures in frames. In one picture a little girl was standing between her mother and her father. Winnie noticed that they had their arms around each other and were smiling.

In the second picture, the girl was older and was riding a horse. The frame had little horseshoes all around it.

"She sure likes horses," said Vanessa.

Zoe turned to Winnie. "What do you want to do?"

Winnie couldn't explain it. She really wanted to

be in the same tent with her friends. But a part of her wanted to stay in this tent, too.

"I'll stay here," she said.

"Are you sure?" asked Vanessa. "It's my turn to be odd girl out. I could stay here if you want."

"No, it's okay," said Winnie. "We're right next door to each other."

The trunks and bags began arriving from the bus. Vanessa and Zoe went to their tent to unpack and Winnie stayed to do the same.

She spread out her sleeping bag and put her pillow at the head of the bed. She took out a raggedy mouse puppet her grandma had given her when she was little and placed it on her pillow. She placed her flashlight, her bug spray, and a locket with a picture of her mother inside on the shelves. Then she stepped back to take a look. Her spot didn't look half as interesting as the area across from hers.

Winnie hunted through her trunk to see if there was anything else she could use to make her

place feel less ordinary. She found a card that she had made the night before with a drawing on the front. It was a self-portrait—a picture of Winnie sitting on the front porch of her house. She had planned to send the drawing to her dad as a surprise. Instead, she duck taped it to the side of her shelves. *There,* she thought. *That helps.*

Winnie was just about to pop into Vanessa and Zoe's tent when Spunky came around to tell her that everyone needed to change into bathing suits for a swim test.

Winnie knew how to swim—all three girls had taken swim lessons at the Y—but she had never had to take a swim "test" before. And she had never before swum in a lake.

"Are there sharks in lakes?" asked Winnie as the girls carried their towels down the path to the waterfront.

"Of course not, Winnie," said Vanessa. "You know that from science class."

"But there are snapping turtles and water moccasins in lakes," said Zoe.

"What are water moccasins?" asked Winnie.

"Snakes," said another girl who was walking just a few feet ahead.

"Snakes?" asked Winnie.

"That's right," said the girl. "Snakes."

Chapter 3

Dolphin, the waterfront counselor, greeted the girls and asked them to jump from the dock into a fairly shallow part of the lake. "Swim your favorite stroke," she said.

The other girls plunged in. Winnie stood on the dock thinking. What was her favorite stroke? Breaststroke? She wasn't that fast at breaststroke. And if there *were* turtles and snakes, she wanted to be fast.

"Can you swim?" asked a lifeguard next to her.

"What?" said Winnie.

"Are you afraid to get into the water?"

No one else was standing on the dock worrying about wildlife. Winnie didn't hesitate any longer.

She jumped into the shallow area, where legs and arms were flailing, and swam a fast freestyle. Within moments, Dolphin tapped her on the shoulder and asked her to stand on the dock again—this time at the deep end.

Vanessa and Zoe were already standing at the end of the dock, shivering but excited.

"Now that we know you can swim," said

Dolphin to the group who had gathered beside Winnie and her friends, "we'd like to see how *long* you can swim. If you can swim for ten minutes without stopping, you'll be permitted to take boats out on your own."

Winnie looked over to where sailboats, canoes, and paddleboats were tied to another dock.

"Okay?" said Dolphin. "Ready, begin."

The girls dove in. Like most of them, Winnie began with freestyle. She noticed that one of the girls, who was wearing a green swim cap, began with the butterfly. *She must be some swimmer,* thought Winnie. *If I began with the butterfly, I'd sink after two minutes.*

After a few laps, Winnie's arms felt heavy, so she switched to the breaststroke. Then she switched to the sidestroke, and then the backstroke. How long had it been? She noticed that there were fewer girls in the swim area and hoped that Vanessa and Zoe were still swimming. She was eager to go boating with them.

To pass the time and to forget about her tired arms, Winnie sang a song in her head. She sang it over and over.

Soap, soap, soap and towel,
Towel and water please.
Merrily, merrily, merrily, merrily,
Wash your dirty knees.

She could hear shouting. It confused her. *Someone must have seen one of those water moccasins,* thought Winnie. Was it near her? She turned over and swam as fast as she could, kicking her feet high in the air. Were water moccasins long like the eels she had seen at the aquarium? Winnie swam even faster.

As she lifted her head to breathe, Winnie could still hear shouting. She treaded water for a moment to discover where it was coming from.

"WINNIE," she heard from behind her.

Winnie turned around in the water and saw all of the girls, standing on the dock.

"Ten minutes was up long ago, love," called Dolphin.

Everyone laughed.

"Oh," said Winnie. She swam toward them and pulled herself up onto the dock.

"Whoeeee! You are some swimmer."

Winnie looked up to see who was talking. It was the butterfly girl. The girl in the green cap. Several girls were standing close to her, as if she were creating a patch of warm sunshine.

"Put it here, Fish," she said.

Winnie slapped the girl's hands and everyone laughed. Even Winnie.

Chapter 4

On their walk back to Treetops, Winnie looked for the girl in the green cap, but she seemed to have disappeared.

Spunky took the girls the long way back, giving them a tour of Camp MacKenzie. She showed them the dining hall, the other camping areas—Ledges, Lily Pads, and Meadows—the arts-and-crafts hut, the horse stables, the archery field, and the infirmary where they would go if hurt or feeling sick.

She also taught the girls a camp song as they walked along—a song that reminded Winnie of the chants that she, Vanessa, and Zoe loved to learn.

"Poor little bug on the wall.
No one to love him at all.
No one to wash his clothes,
  no one to tickle his toes—
Poor little bug on the wall!"

Winnie and Zoe were still singing the song when they reached Treetops.

"Shhh!" said Vanessa.

"What's wrong?" whispered Winnie. She didn't like the look on Vanessa's face.

"There's something in your tent," said Vanessa. "I can hear it."

A bear, thought Winnie. She had read about bears and how they would come into camps, searching for something to eat. She was glad that her father insisted she follow the camp rule printed in capital letters on the "Things to Bring" list: NO FOOD.

Suddenly the flap of the tent flew open. The girls jumped back.

"Hi, Fish!"

It was the girl in the green bathing cap.

"Are you the girl with horses on her bed?" asked Zoe.

"That would be me," said the girl. She had dancing curly hair and freckles.

Winnie spoke up, "I'm in this tent, too. I'm Winnie. And this is Vanessa and Zoe." She wanted to tell her that they were three best friends, but something stopped her.

"I'm Roxie," said the girl. "And this is Nora and

Nell," she added, pointing through the open flap. Winnie could see that her two other tent mates had arrived. They were identical twins, sitting on identically made beds.

Both the girls gave a quick smile.

Winnie smiled back.

"We better go and change," said Vanessa. "We'll see you later, Winnie."

It felt funny staying behind. She entered the tent, changed her clothes, and began a letter to her dad. She told him that she was in a different tent from Vanessa and Zoe. But she also told him about her friend Roxie. She knew that she and Roxie weren't *really* friends, at least not yet, but she didn't want her dad to worry about her.

"I live on a ranch," she heard Roxie say to the twins.

"Wow!" said Nell. "I've never met anyone who lived on a real ranch before."

"Do you have a horse?" asked Nora.

"Sure do," said Roxie. "His name is Skipsy."

"You're so lucky," said Nora. "All we have are guppies."

"I'm an equestrian," said Roxie.

"What's an equestrian?" asked Nell.

"Someone who rides horses."

"Wow," said Nell. "Are you in horse shows and everything? That's so glamorous."

"Do you jump?" asked Nora. "Is it scary?"

Roxie told them all about the time she made her first show jump with Skipsy.

Winnie sat down on her bed and listened. Unlike Nora and Nell, she couldn't think of a single bingle thing to say. Every time she opened her mouth, a little voice inside her head said *Don't say that! That's stupid.*

"Hey, what's this?" asked Roxie. She was pointing to the picture that Winnie had drawn.

Winnie wished she had kept the drawing in her trunk.

"That's you," said Roxie. "Kazoo, kazak! It looks

exactly like you. Where did you learn how to draw like this?"

Winnie had always liked to draw. It was simply something she did. But that sounded so boring. Instead, Winnie found herself saying something completely unexpected. "From my mother."

"Wow. Is your mother an artist?" asked Nell.

"Is she famous?" asked Nora.

"Sort of," said Winnie, not knowing where the words were coming from.

"I bet she's a great artist, Fish," said Roxie, "if she's half as good as you."

Winnie felt a smile carve into her face. She liked being called Fish by Roxie.

And she loved that Roxie had liked her drawing. Normally Winnie would carry a compliment like that around with her for a full week, like a sparkly white rock in her pocket, ready to pull out and feel warm against her skin at any time.

Only this time, Winnie couldn't enjoy the compliment for long. Because there were other thoughts, harsh thoughts, that were piling up like a hill of granite boulders.

Well, my mother was, Winnie thought, trying to push away those heavy thoughts. *My mother was an artist—sort of. Dad has a painting she did hanging on his bedroom wall. And she might have been famous one day, too. If she hadn't died after I was born.*

Chapter 5

"That's the dinner bell," said Roxie. "Let's go." She jumped off the tent platform and started up the path. Nora and Nell ran to catch up.

Winnie wasn't sure what to do. Should she see about Vanessa and Zoe? Or catch up to Roxie too? Spunky and another counselor were moving from tent to tent, gathering girls to lead them to the dining hall.

Winnie decided to wait outside her tent. At school, Vanessa, Zoe, and she were in different classes, but they always waited for one another at the beginning of recess or when school was over.

Then she saw Spunky peek into Vanessa and Zoe's tent and call to the other counselor, whose name was Star, "These girls have already gone."

Gone? Vanessa and Zoe went to dinner without her? Would they be at the dining hall? Who would she sit with?

Winnie tagged along with girls from other tents. She didn't know if any of them were first-time campers. She tried to figure out who were friends from home and who were camp friends and who had just met, but all the girls sounded happy and excited and as if they'd known each other for a million years.

To get to the dining hall, the girls walked on a trail that wound past the infirmary, past the waterfront, and past Lily Pads, where the younger campers stayed.

The Treetops girls were the last to arrive, and so they were the very last campers in line. A second bell rang, the double doors of the dining hall opened, and the girls flooded through. Winnie looked around madly. Most of the tables were filled. She spotted Vanessa and Zoe sitting at a table with one chair available, and darted over.

"That's the hopper's seat," said a girl seated at the table. "It's not available."

Zoe made a sad face.

"There's a seat behind us," said a counselor.

Winnie moved to one of two empty seats at the next table.

"You're sitting in the Cinderella seat," said a girl who was slightly older than Winnie.

Winnie had no idea who or what the hopper was. And did she need to leave the Cinderella seat? Or did sitting in the seat make her Cinderella? And what did that mean? She stayed seated in the Cinderella seat, wondering what else she wouldn't know at Camp MacKenzie.

Grace, for one thing. The girls sang a thank-you song that Winnie had never heard before. Then they began to pass the food.

"Hey, Winnie," said a voice behind her. Winnie

turned to see Roxie carrying a big bowl of spaghetti to the empty seat next to Winnie's. Roxie then went back to the kitchen and returned with a bowl of steaming sauce. "I'm the hopper," she said. "I have to hop up and down to bring food and drinks to the table." She sat down next to Winnie.

Winnie couldn't believe her luck. Roxie had come to her rescue once again.

"Don't forget the bread," the counselor said, and Roxie hopped back up again.

The food was passed from camper to camper. Winnie loved spaghetti and felt like she could eat the whole bowl, but was careful to see how much the other campers were placing on their plates.

"What's the Cinderella seat?" Winnie asked Roxie when she had brought all the food to the table.

"The girl in the Cinderella seat has to stay after dinner and help sweep the dining room."

Sweep? Where would she find a broom? Winnie wanted to ask Roxie more questions about the Cinderella job. How long did she need to stay? Where would the other campers be while she swept?

But Roxie was busy talking to other girls. All of the girls, except for one that looked younger than Winnie, seemed to know Roxie.

"Are you going to rock climb this year?" a girl in braids asked Roxie.

"I couldn't believe that you climbed the ledge last year," said another. "It's the steepest climb and you were only eight!"

"Have you ever gone rock climbing?" the counselor asked Winnie and the younger girl. Winnie knew that she was trying to help them be part of the conversation.

Both Winnie and the girl shook their heads.

"I'll show you how. There's really nothing to it," said Roxie.

"That's what *you* say!" said the girl with braids. Everyone laughed.

"Picasso," said Roxie, speaking to the counselor at the table. "You should see Fish here draw."

Roxie turned to Winnie and said, "Picasso's the arts-and-crafts counselor."

"I'd love to see you draw," said Picasso as she took the last of the salad from a bowl. "I hope you'll come to the arts-and-crafts cabin often."

"Her mom's a famous artist," said Roxie.

"Is that right?" asked Picasso. She looked right at Winnie now. "What's her name?"

Winnie thought frantically. Should she say her mother's name? Make up a name? Fortunately, Winnie didn't get a chance to answer. The whole dining room broke out into song:

"Save your forks,
Save your forks,
For dessert, for dessert.
We'll have something yummy,
Yummy for the tummy,
For dessert."

When the song ended, Picasso seemed to have forgotten her question.

Dessert was chocolate cake with white frosting. The girls were allowed two pieces.

"Hey, I'll help you sweep," said Roxie when the meal had ended.

Winnie smiled. She had never met anyone like Roxie before.

The dining room cleared out and Roxie took her to the closet, where they each got a broom.

"*I said broom chicka-broom!*" sang a familiar voice behind them.

"Ha!" said Winnie. Vanessa had unknowingly taken a Cinderella seat, too. Winnie almost asked, "How come you guys didn't wait for me?" but it didn't seem to matter any longer.

Winnie started sweeping up strands of spaghetti, bits of lettuce, and chocolate crumbs. She thought about the counselors she'd met so far. Winnie liked that they had names that matched their personalities or interests: Spunky *was* spunky, Dolphin loved the water, and Picasso had the name of a famous artist. She wondered if they had picked the names themselves.

The corner where Winnie was sweeping began to look clean. She looked over at Vanessa talking

to Roxie and tried to imagine what they were talking about.

Why were Roxie's eyebrows going up in that way? Suddenly Winnie felt as if she were breathing in all the dust she'd swept. *Please don't let Vanessa and Roxie be talking about me,* she thought. *Me and my famous mom.*

Chapter 6

That night the girls gathered around the campfire to play name games. At first Winnie, Vanessa, and Zoe sat next to one another. But they were separated by the Spunky and Star and placed with other girls during the games so that they could get to know all the Treetops campers.

Roxie knew the games and even suggested that they play a new one—the shoe game. Each girl placed one sneaker or sandal in a pile. When Spunky said "Go!" the girls ran and chose a shoe that belonged to someone else. Then they had to find the owner of the shoe and learn the girl's name.

It turned out that Winnie had chosen Nora's sneaker.

"You'll know Nora's sneakers really well by the time camp ends," said Nell, holding her nose.

Nora pretended to punch Nell.

Winnie laughed.

"Here's yours, Fish," said Roxie. She held out a gray-and-blue sneaker.

"That's not Winnie's sneaker," said Vanessa. "This one is!" Vanessa also held a gray-and-blue sneaker, only hers was larger.

"That sneaker is mine," said Vanessa, taking the sneaker that Roxie held.

"You guys have the same sneakers?" asked Roxie.

"Yup," said Vanessa. "We bought them together. Only Winnie's are about three sizes larger."

"I can't help it if I have big feet," said Winnie.

"Big feet, big brains, that's what I always say," said Roxie holding her foot up to Winnie's. Roxie's foot was the same size.

Vanessa put her missing sneaker on and jumped up onto a large tree stump.

"Ladies and"—Vanessa put her hand above her eyes and pretended to scan a large crowd—"ladies," she said.

Winnie and Roxie looked up at her. So did Zoe and some of the other girls.

"Is it true," asked Vanessa, "that big feet equal—" But before she could finish her sentence, she tumbled off the back of the stump.

"Vanessa!" shouted Winnie.

"Vanessa, are you all right?" asked Zoe.

Vanessa did not seem all right. She crouched close to the ground, holding her ankle. Winnie could tell that she was trying hard not to cry.

Star came running. She had Vanessa sit on the stump and looked to see if her ankle was swelling. It didn't seem to be, but when Vanessa tried to stand, she cringed.

"I'll take her to the infirmary," said Roxie.

"That's probably a good idea," said Star. "We'll have Nurse check her out."

"Come on, Tumbledown," said Roxie. She put Vanessa's arm around her shoulder and the two of them started off down the path, Vanessa hopping on one foot. They wobbled to one side and then the other and then had to stop because they were laughing so hard.

"Time to get ready for bed," said Star when the girls had gone.

Everyone else besides Vanessa and Roxie went to their cabins, grabbed their flashlights, and slid out metal white washbasins from under their beds. They carried the washbasins down to the "trough," a long sink filled with many spigots, to fill them with water. Then they used the basins to brush their teeth and wash their faces. The girls took turns shining their lights under the outhouse door for one another, then headed back up to their tents.

Winnie and Zoe walked up the hill to the tents together. "What should we do tomorrow?" asked Winnie. They had been told that they could choose their own activities at camp—they were even allowed to make up an activity, as long as they could talk a counselor into helping them.

"Let's go to the arts-and-crafts hut first," said Zoe. "I want to weave."

Winnie could tell by the sound of Zoe's voice

that she was feeling lonely. Zoe, she guessed, was lonesome for Vanessa, the only person in her tent that she knew well. And Winnie, as strange as it seemed, wished that she had been the one to twist her ankle.

Chapter 7

The following morning, the girls were prepared. Roxie, Vanessa (whose ankle had not been badly hurt), Zoe, and Winnie left their tents as soon as they heard the first breakfast bell. They stood together at the base of the dining hall stairs, first in line. When the second bell rang, they burst through the double doors and found seats at the same table. No one sat in the Cinderella seat.

Announcements followed every meal. The counselors presented the day's activities. Spunky said that she would be doing tie-dye T-shirts at Treetops. Star would teach rock climbing. Dolphin was having water relays at the swimming dock, and Picasso said that she would be teaching the girls how to use a pottery wheel this week.

As the girls left the dining hall, Vanessa said, "I have to go back to the infirmary this morning. Nurse wants to make sure my ankle's still okay after a night's sleep." She looked at Roxie, hoping, Winnie knew, that Roxie would offer to go with her again.

"We're heading to arts and crafts, right, Win?" asked Zoe.

"But I thought I was going to teach you to rock climb, Fish," said Roxie.

"You were serious?" asked Winnie. "I thought you were just being nice."

Vanessa looked disappointed.

"No, I meant it," said Roxie. "I'll help you get to the top of the ledge before the morning is through."

"Do you want to rock climb, Zoe?" asked Winnie.

Zoe looked down. "No, I'll go with Vanessa to the infirmary."

"Are you sure, Zoe?" asked Winnie. "I could rock climb another time."

"No, go ahead," said Zoe. *I know rock climbing with Roxie is what you really want to do,* were the unspoken words that everyone knew Zoe was thinking.

"Save me a seat at lunch," Winnie said to Vanessa and Zoe, and followed Roxie on a dirt path that led to several large boulders at the base of a steep rock ledge. There were also many rope courses at the base of the ledge, to help the girls develop stronger muscles and coordination for climbing.

"Hey, Star," said Roxie.

"Hey there, Miss Climber," said Star.

Star was carrying harnesses that the girls would wear. The harnesses were attached to ropes—ropes that would hold the girls up if they fell. Behind Star came several other girls eager to try rock climbing.

Roxie showed Winnie how to put a harness on

and how to search for hand- and footholds. Star came over and made sure the rope was securely connected to Winnie's harness and then she held the rope so that Winnie could start to climb.

Winnie found a place to put her feet and hands and hoisted herself onto the boulder. Roxie cheered her on, but Winnie could hardly hear her as she looked for a foothold, then a handhold, then a foothold again. Just once, she stopped to imagine what would happen if she slipped. She became wobbly thinking about it. Her knees began to shake.

"Just think about going up," yelled Star.

Winnie put thoughts of falling (along with scrapes, cuts, and bruises) out of her mind and continued moving to the top. The hardest spot was the top. There seemed to be no place to put her hands and she didn't know if she had the strength to pull herself onto the rock. *I can't do this*, she thought.

"Come on, Fish! Crawl to the top. You won't fall."

Winnie raised one foot to a high foothold and began crawling onto the top of the boulder. It worked! "Wow," she said, standing up. "The boulder doesn't look this high from the bottom."

Both Roxie and Star laughed.

To get off the boulder, Winnie simply had to slide down the back side, which wasn't nearly as steep as the front.

Roxie said, "Let's climb the ledge."

"Winnie may not be ready to climb the ledge yet," said Star. "Remember, this is her first time." Then she turned to Winnie and said, "Perhaps you'd like to try some of the other boulders or a rope course."

Winnie looked at the ledge. It was straight up and down. A rock wall. "You go first, then I'll decide," she said to Roxie.

Star held the ropes for Roxie, who stretched her body as far as it could reach to find one foothold or handhold after another. Winnie gasped a couple times when it looked as if Roxie would slip or dangle in midair. But Roxie didn't seem scared and she didn't slow down once before reaching the top.

"I'll go," said Winnie.

"Are you sure?" asked Star.

Winnie nodded.

The climb to the top was much harder than Roxie made it look. Winnie stood in one place for a long time, thinking about where to put her hands and feet next. She knew that she had a harness on, she knew that the rope could catch her, but for some reason it didn't make her feel safer.

The day was hot and her hands began to sweat. A fly buzzed around her head. The noise irritated Winnie, and she tried to swat the fly as she reached for the next handhold, but that made her slide a little. She grabbed on again and took a deep breath. Again, her knees began to shake.

Maybe she should just climb back down. But then she thought of Roxie at the top of the ledge. What would Roxie think if she chickened out? Would she still want her as a friend? Winnie wasn't sure.

She reached for the next handhold and pulled herself higher. Then another and another.

"You're doing it!" yelled someone from below.

Roxie held her hand down to Winnie and Winnie took it. She made it! She'd climbed the ledge on her very first try.

From the top, Winnie could see the whole lake, the horse stables, and the field with the archery targets and arts-and-crafts hut.

"Halloooo!" called Winnie.

"Kazoo, kazak!" called Roxie.

"If only my father could see me now," whispered Winnie.

"Would he be surprised?"

Winnie nodded. "I'm a klutz," she said, willing to admit this now that she'd made it to the top.

"My dad wouldn't be surprised. He calls me his monkey. What about your mother?"

"What?" asked Winnie.

"Your mother. What will your mother say when you tell her that you climbed the ledge?"

Winnie had almost forgotten her lie. She quickly thought of several possibilities—things that her mother might have said—and then chose the one she liked best.

"She'll say, 'I knew you could do it!'" said Winnie.

"I wish I had *your* mom," said Roxie. "My mother will say, 'Did the counselor check to make sure your harness was tight? Did you wear your hiking shoes? Did you remember your sunscreen?'"

Winnie laughed. She knew Roxie was probably exaggerating, but even if Roxie's mom did say all those things, Winnie thought they sounded kind of nice.

Chapter 8

"Hey, let's do a floating lunch!" said Roxie as she and Winnie walked back down the path toward the dining hall.

"What's a floating lunch?"

"Follow me and I'll show you," said Roxie.

She led Winnie around to the back door of the dining hall, where the kitchen was located, and knocked.

"Hi, Cookie!" Roxie said to a woman who came to the door wearing a white apron.

"Well, hello, Roxie. Nice to see you back!"

"Cookie, could Fish and I have bag lunches for a floating lunch?"

"You know that you need to arrange for a bag lunch at breakfast, Roxie."

"I know," said Roxie. "But I just thought of a floating lunch and it's such a hot day. It would be the perfect thing!"

"I suppose you're right about that," said Cookie. "I'll see what I can do." She disappeared from the door.

"She's so nice," said Winnie.

"She is," said Roxie. "That gives me an idea. Wait here."

Winnie felt nervous sitting out by the kitchen door by herself. She hoped the camp director or a counselor wouldn't come by and ask her what she was doing. She didn't want to get in trouble on her first full day. And she didn't want to get Cookie in trouble either.

Roxie came running back with a pencil and a napkin she'd found in the front part of the dining hall. "Draw a picture of Cookie," said Roxie.

"But I only saw her for a moment," said Winnie. "And she was behind the screen door."

"That's okay," said Roxie. "It doesn't have to look exactly like her."

Winnie took the pencil and drew a woman with her hair in a bun wearing a white apron. She added a big wooden spoon to her hand for fun. It didn't look too bad for a quick sketch.

Roxie took the napkin back and wrote THANK YOU, COOKIE in big letters beneath the picture. When Cookie came back holding two paper bags, Roxie handed her the napkin.

"What's this?" Cookie said, and laughed. "I didn't know you could draw, Roxie."

"I didn't draw it, Fish did."

Cookie looked at Winnie. "You are so talented—um—Fish, is it? I'm going to pin this up on my bulletin board."

"Fish's mother is a famous artist," said Roxie.

"Well, I predict you will be one day, too," said Cookie turning to go back inside. "Have fun on your floating lunch."

Roxie led Winnie back to Treetops, where they changed into bathing suits and got their white washbasins. Then she led her to the waterfront.

"What are you doing here?" asked Dolphin.

"May we have a floating lunch?" asked Roxie.

Dolphin sighed. "You're in luck," she said. "I was going to eat in the dining hall today, but another bunch of girls asked to have a picnic on the docks. So I guess it will be all right if you float nearby."

Roxie showed Winnie how to put on an orange life jacket that was normally used for boating. Then they placed their brown-bag lunches into the basins, slid off the docks into the deep end, and turned back to retrieve their lunches off the dock. The lunches floated around in their

own little white boats, while Winnie and Roxie paddled after them.

Cookie had packed a scrumpdillyitious lunch, and as Winnie floated on her back, looked up at the blue sky, and munched on a chicken salad sandwich (only slightly soggy), she couldn't remember having more fun.

What she didn't remember while drifting along sipping her juice and eating chocolate chip cookies was that she had asked Zoe and Vanessa to save her a seat at lunch.

"What happened to you guys?" shouted Vanessa from her open tent flap when Winnie and Roxie returned for rest period.

"What do you mean?" asked Roxie.

"We saved you seats," said Zoe. "Which our counselor was not happy about."

"And when you didn't show up, we were sure one of you got killed on the rocks," said Vanessa.

"We went for a floating lunch," said Roxie.

"You guys won't believe what that is," said Winnie excitedly. "You put on a life jacket, put your lunch in—"

"Save it, Winnie," said Vanessa, turning her back on her. "I'd rather finish my letter right now."

Zoe went back to her writing too.

Chapter 9

"What's up with Tumbledown and Zo-Zo?" asked Roxie when they were resting on their beds.

Winnie paused.

"They're not used to me doing something different from what I said I'd do," said Winnie, who had never thought about it before, but knew it was the honest truth.

"That's weird," said Roxie. "People change their minds."

That's true. People do change their minds, thought Winnie. *Maybe it* is *weird that Vanessa and Zoe are mad.*

"Did I tell you that Vanessa, Zoe, and I belong to the End-of-the-Alphabet Club?" said Winnie, wanting Roxie to understand how things were with her two best friends.

"Huh?" said Roxie.

"All of our names begin with a letter that is at the end of the alphabet," said Winnie.

"That's cool," said Nora who was playing a game of cards with her sister.

"V, W, and Z!" said Nell. "You just need an X and a Y for additional members."

"Hey, maybe I could be in your club!" said Roxie. "I have an X smack in the middle of my name."

Winnie smiled a half smile. She had no idea what Zoe and Vanessa would say to that.

And she didn't have a chance to ask them, because by the time rest period ended and Winnie had closed the mystery she was reading, Vanessa and Zoe had already headed down the camp path without even telling Winnie where they were going.

"Hey, Roxie, want to come with me to the horse

barn?" asked a girl named Madeline. Two other girls were standing in back of her.

"Sure," said Roxie, who put away her stationery and then jumped from the tent platform to the ground. The girls started toward the path.

Winnie looked at Nell and Nora.

"We're going to try archery this afternoon," said Nell.

"That sounds fun," said Winnie.

"Do you want to come?" asked Nora.

Winnie felt a little better when Nora asked her, but she also felt tired from rock climbing and swimming. She didn't think she'd have much success standing in a hot field trying to hit a target with a flying arrow. "No, thanks," she said. "I think I might try the arts-and-crafts hut."

It felt strange walking down the path to the hut on her own. For a moment, she wished that she were back on Clementine Street with her dad.

Winnie heard voices coming from the hut and wondered whether she should continue. What if there were a bunch of older campers inside? She could wander around camp—maybe she would bump into Vanessa and Zoe—but camp was a pretty big place. She pushed open the door.

The art room at school looked nothing like this! On the shelves was every kind of art supply imaginable. There were tubes of paints, bottles of paints, and watercolor sets. There was origami paper, tissue paper, and construction paper of every color. Below the papers were yarns for weaving, floss for embroidery, and multicolored strings. Winnie felt as if she'd just walked into the candy store of her dreams.

Along the walls were looms for weaving, easels for painting, and several potter's wheels. Several girls were at the wheels preparing to make pots. Picasso was helping the girls dig clay out of a big barrel.

All of the pottery wheels were taken, but Winnie was happy just to poke around. On the walls were prints done by famous artists, and paintings or

drawings done by campers. Winnie could tell that the campers had different abilities, but in this hut every piece of art looked like a masterpiece. In one corner was a calendar with a different painting for each month. Winnie's favorite was August:

a picture of owls by a woman named Ann Hunt.

"Well, hello," said Picasso to Winnie. "You're Fish, aren't you?"

Winnie didn't know how to answer so she just nodded her head.

"As you can see, the wheels are taken, but is there something else you would like to do?"

Winnie pointed to an open drawer that had colored pencils, pastels, and charcoal inside. "May I draw with charcoal, please?" she asked.

"Why, of course," said Picasso. "She took out a sheet of white paper for Winnie and set it on one of the big tables in the center of the room.

Winnie drew a picture of an owl hidden in the shadows of a tree. The charcoal allowed her to show that it was night and the owl's eyes were the brightest spot on her picture.

"Oooh! That's wonderful!" said Picasso, peering over her shoulder when Winnie had finished. "Now I remember. Your mother is an artist. What did you tell me her name was?"

For a second time, Winnie didn't know what to do with this question. Should she make up a name? Add a lie to a lie? Picasso was waiting for an answer. Winnie said the first name that popped into her head. "Ann Hunt."

"Your mother is Ann Hunt!" Picasso was clearly amazed. "Why, I've admired her work for years." She looked back at Winnie's picture. "Of course! I see your mother's influence!"

Winnie wished that she could vanish into the dark branches that surrounded the owl.

"You'll have to tell your mother that I love her work. Oh, I can't wait to meet her on Visitors' Day."

Chapter 10

First in line for dinner, Winnie decided to take a hopper seat. She hoped that Vanessa and Zoe would choose her table, but when the rest of the campers rushed in, a group of girls from Lily Pads took all the seats.

After dinner, the whole camp stayed at the dining hall for a sing-along. Winnie found Roxie and sat down beside her, but wondered where Vanessa and Zoe had gone.

The next morning, Zoe wandered over to Winnie's tent. Winnie's heart jumped to see her. "Vanessa and I are going back to arts and crafts this morning. I want to work on my weaving. Would you like to come?"

Winnie was about to say, "Yes, yes, yessiree!" when she remembered her conversation with Picasso. No doubt Picasso would say something about Winnie's mother.

"I can't," said Winnie, but as she tried to come up with a reason why, Zoe turned to leave.

"I didn't think so, but I thought I'd ask anyway," Zoe said.

Winnie didn't know what to do. Should she run after Zoe and explain the true reason why she couldn't go to arts and crafts? But the next moment, Roxie asked Winnie if she'd like to hike with a group to Slippery Falls, where the girls could ride the waterfalls like playground slides. Winnie thought that this hike sounded magical. Maybe it was better that she had told Zoe that she couldn't go to arts and crafts, after all.

The hike was perfect. It wasn't so short that Winnie felt as if she'd taken a walk around her own back yard. It wasn't so long that she wished a flying carpet would come and swoop her to the end. And the falls *were* magical. Roxie and Winnie would sit at the top of a misty waterfall and slip-slide around bends until they plunged together into a cool pool at the end of each one.

On the hike back, the girls talked about their pets and the silly things that they could do.

Madeline had a dog that sang whenever someone in her family played a musical instrument. Another girl had a real ferret that would sit upon her shoulder. Roxie told about Skipsy, and how he seemed to smile whenever Roxie walked into the barn.

Before she knew it, Winnie was telling about her imaginary cat, Mr. Edgar, and how he would prowl around her neighborhood, looking for treasures.

"What kind of treasures?" asked Madeline, who seemed not to believe Winnie.

"Oh, the silver paper from gum wrappers, or a cloth elastic that had fallen out of someone's hair, that sort of thing," said Winnie, who at that moment almost believed the story herself.

"Who would want those things?" asked a girl with blond braids.

"My mother," said Winnie. "She uses that sort of thing in her art."

"Cool," said Roxie.

That night, all of the girls were sitting around the campfire, eating s'mores—one of Winnie's favorite foods.

"I'm finishing my weaving tomorrow," said Zoe. "Do you want to come with us to arts and crafts and see?"

"Hey, Fish," said Roxie. "We *should* go to arts

and crafts. We could weave a collar for Mr. Edgar."

"Mr. Edgar?" asked Vanessa.

"You know," said Roxie. "Winnie's cat."

"Winnie doesn't have a—"

"A *bit* of weaving talent," said Winnie.

Vanessa tried again. "That's not—"

"*True,*" said Winnie. "Yes it is."

Vanessa looked at Winnie and didn't say one word more.

That is, until they were washing up that evening. Winnie was sitting in the outhouse when she overhead Vanessa talking to Zoe. She couldn't hear everything Vanessa was saying, but she was quite certain she heard three words: Big Fat Liar.

Chapter 11

Winnie lay on her cot at rest hour. The morning had not gone well. When she had told Vanessa and Zoe that she *would* like to go to arts and crafts with them that morning, they told her that they had changed their minds and signed up for the hike to Slippery Falls. Campers could only sign up for this hike once.

Roxie, Winnie had discovered, was going down to the stables. Trotter, the horseback-riding counselor, was going to take a group of advanced riders out onto the trails. Winnie was not an advanced rider.

Nora and Nell had already left for the archery fields again.

So much for being a natural-born camper, Winnie thought. She had no idea what to do. Finally, she threw on the cut-off shorts her dad had made and headed to the arts and crafts hut on her own.

Picasso was so preoccupied with potters and weavers that she hardly paid any attention to Winnie, drawing in the corner. At first Winnie was glad that Picasso was so busy. But by the end of activity time, Winnie wished that Picasso had talked to her just once, even if all she gushed about was Winnie's imaginary mother.

Back at the tent, Winnie looked up at the ceiling and sang to herself,

"Poor little bug on the wall.
No one to love him at all.
No one to wash his clothes,
   no one to tickle his toes—
Poor little bug on the wall!"

It was just a silly camp song, but it made Winnie feel sad. She thought about Vanessa's words: Big fat liar. Was she a liar? She *had* told a lot of lies at camp. Somehow she couldn't stop herself. *Maybe*, thought Winnie, *maybe I have some sort of lying disease.*

"Mail for Winnie Fletcher!" said Spunky as she poked her head in the tent and handed Winnie a letter. Winnie recognized the handwriting immediately.

Hi Winner,
I got your letter today. It sounds
like you're having a great time
at camp. Guess what! I have good
news. I was able to find someone
to teach my class on Saturday.
That means I will be able to come
to camp on Visitors' Day. I'll
be coming with Vanessa's family.

*Can't wait to see you and meet
your new friend Roxie.*

> *Lots of love,*
> *Dad*

"Kazoo, kazak!" shouted
Winnie.

"Hey, you sound like me,"
said Roxie, who had just
returned, covered in dust
from the stables.

"My dad's coming for
Visitors' Day!"

"I didn't know that he
wasn't coming," said Roxie.
"Is your mom coming, too?"

"No," said Winnie. "She has—uh—an art show."

"Who has an art show?" asked Vanessa, pop-
ping over from her tent to borrow Nora and
Nell's cards.

"Winnie's—"

"Come with me," said Winnie, grabbing Vanessa's arm and pulling her down toward the water trough. "I want to tell you about my letter."

"Winnie!" yelled Vanessa. "Zoe and I are about to play cards!"

"It's rest period," called Spunky from her tent. "You girls are supposed to be doing quiet activities."

"Wait here," whispered Winnie. "I'll go get Zoe."

"I can't believe this," said Vanessa, but she sat down on a rock near the trough and waited anyway.

"What is it?" asked Zoe when she and Winnie reached Vanessa's rock.

"My dad. He's coming for Visitors' Day."

"Is that all?" asked Vanessa. "Why didn't you say that at the tent?"

Winnie sighed. How could she tell her friends? "I thought it would be great," she said. "But it's not. It's horrible."

"Horrible?" Zoe looked confused.

Winnie led the girls closer to the lake so that the other girls wouldn't overhear them.

"It's just that Roxie and some of the counselors and, well, even some of the other girls think that—" Winnie paused to decide what she should say next.

"I knew it!" said Vanessa. "You've been lying to them. Just so they'd like you better than us."

"That's not true!" said Winnie. "I didn't want them to like me better than you, I just didn't want—" How could she say this? "I just didn't want to be the different one."

"What do you mean?" asked Vanessa. "What makes you so different?"

"Well," said Winnie. She ran her hand up a stem of a fern, which left her holding a leaf bouquet. "Not having a mother makes me different."

"Lots of kids don't live with their mothers," said Vanessa.

"I know," said Winnie, tossing the leaves into the air. "But people treat you differently when they find out your mother is dead."

"You told them that your mother is *alive?*" asked Zoe.

"Well, I didn't actually say that," said Winnie. "Not at first." She paused. "But I did let them *think* that."

"And what else?" asked Vanessa. "Besides the fact that you have a cat named Mr. Edgar."

Winnie took a deep breath and huffed it out. "That my mom is a famous artist named Ann Hunt."

Vanessa opened her eyes wide.

Zoe sat down at the edge of the lake. "What are you going to do?" she asked.

"I don't know exactly," said Winnie. "But would you help me?"

"Help!" Vanessa was nearly shouting again. "You haven't done a single activity with us and now you want us to help you?"

"I know," said Winnie. She searched for just the right words. The true words. "It wasn't that I didn't want to be with you. I guess I haven't really known how to be a best friend here at camp." It was the most honest thing that Winnie had said in days. And it felt good to say it.

Chapter 12

To work on their plan, Winnie, Vanessa, and Zoe found a time to sneak away each day until Saturday, Visitors' Day. Vanessa and Zoe had stopped being mad at Winnie. In fact, it seemed as if everyone was happier now that they had a reason to plan together. Winnie was the happiest (and the most grateful) of all.

Zoe got a copy of the Visitors' Day schedule from Spunky:

10–11	Parents and friends arrive
11–12	Tour of the camp
12–1	Barbecue
1–2	All-camp relay races

Sitting on the dock on Thursday during lunch, the girls tried to come up with a way to keep Mr. Fletcher away from Roxie and Picasso, the two people most likely to say something about Winnie's famous mother. But it seemed nearly impossible.

"Maybe I should just tell them the truth," said Winnie, "before my father arrives."

"They might understand," said Zoe, taking the lettuce out of her tuna fish sandwich and feeding it to a duck that was swimming nearby.

"Or be really mad," said Vanessa. "I hate it when someone lies to me. I feel like they're making fun of me."

Winnie knew what Vanessa meant. She felt like a fool when she found out that lemonade did *not* come out of the sixth-grade water fountain like the older students told her it did.

Winnie thought about Roxie and all the fun they'd had together so far. She didn't want to hurt Roxie's feelings. And she definitely didn't want Roxie to be mad at her.

She couldn't tell the truth.

On Friday, the girls took a rowboat out into the middle of the lake and floated while they schemed. Winnie wrote a plan on her camp stationery:

> 1. Take our parents on the tour quickly so we get ahead of Roxie and the other girls.

2. Vanessa will keep on the lookout for Roxie and distract her if she comes near.

3. Zoe will talk to Picasso when we come to the arts-and-crafts hut so Picasso won't get a chance to talk to my dad.

It seemed like a good plan. A plan that just might work.

Chapter 13

The girls were told to clean up their tents and themselves before visitors arrived. They rushed through chores and then tried to get brushes through their seldom-combed hair. Vanessa's long curly hair was the hardest to work with, and all the campers, including Vanessa and Zoe's two other tent mates, took turns trying to pull a brush through.

"Ouch!" cried Vanessa when it was Winnie's turn.

"Sorry," said Winnie. "I'm having a hard time paying attention to anything this morning."

At ten, campers congregated near the dining hall to wait for visitors.

"There's my mother!" said Roxie. "Now I just have to wait for my father and my stepmother."

"You didn't tell us that your parents were divorced," said Nora.

"You didn't ask," said Roxie.

Winnie wondered if not telling was the same as lying. She doubted it. Roxie hadn't said that her father was a movie star or something.

Zoe's parents were the next to arrive. Then dozens of other cars pulled up (or so it seemed to Winnie).

Finally the Wiley van, belonging to Vanessa's family, pulled in. The girls ran to meet their families.

"Winner!" said Mr. Fletcher as he pulled himself out of the back of the van. Winnie leaped into his arms.

"Come on!" shouted Vanessa to the grownups and her little sister,

Marissa. "We have to get going on the tour!"

The girls began the tour at Treetops. From there they rushed to the swimming area, and the boating docks, and then climbed the hill to the infirmary, so that Vanessa could show them where she'd had her ankle wrapped. "Slow down!" begged Mrs. Wiley, who was pulling little Marissa by the hand.

Nurse was alone, and happy to chat with the parents as they caught their breath. She showed them around the infirmary and talked about times when campers broke their wrists or ate too much at the summer taffy pull. As the group was preparing to leave, Nurse said to Mr. Fletcher, "Picasso is a friend of mine. She has been telling me all about the work of Ann Hunt."

Mr. Fletcher looked at Nurse, clearly waiting to hear more.

Zoe made a worried face and quickly led her parents out of the infirmary. Vanessa followed.

"Picasso is the arts-and-crafts instructor," said Winnie. "Come on, let's catch up!"

"Winnie," said Mr. Fletcher as the group started back down the hill. "That was rude. What was Nurse saying about Ann somebody?"

"Who knows," said Winnie. "Come on, I want to show you the rock-climbing course!"

Winnie should have known better. "Hey, Fish!" yelled a voice when the group arrived. Winnie looked up and saw Roxie standing on the tallest boulder. Star was holding the ropes, helping

Roxie demonstrate rock climbing for her family.

Vanessa dutifully began talking to Roxie, just as they had planned. "How long did it take you to climb that boulder?" she asked, sounding like a newspaper reporter.

"Not long," said Roxie. "This one's not that hard."

"Keep holding on to the rope," shouted Roxie's mom.

Actually, thought Winnie, *this might be the perfect time to introduce Dad to Roxie. She can't say much standing up on the boulder.*

"Roxie, this is my father. Dad, this is my friend Roxie that I told you about."

"Hi, Mr. Fish!" said Roxie.

"Did she say Mr. *Fish*?" Mr. Fletcher asked Winnie in a low voice.

"Oh! So *you're* Fish!" said Roxie's father, patting Winnie on the head. "We've heard so much about you." Then he held out his hand and introduced himself to Mr. Fletcher. The two had barely spoken two words when Winnie said, "See you, Roxie, we have to finish the tour," and pulled her father away.

"Winnie!" said Mr. Fletcher.

"I'm so glad you could come today, Dad," said Winnie, squeezing his hand.

Mr. Fletcher smiled and Winnie knew that the moment for the manners lecture had passed.

Winnie held her breath when they got to the arts-and-crafts hut. This was going to be the most difficult part of the tour. "Do you want to wait out here?" asked Winnie. "It's awfully hot in the hut sometimes."

"I don't mind the heat," said Mr. Fletcher. "Besides, if I know *you*, you've spent a lot of time in there."

Winnie and Mr. Fletcher walked in. Zoe had already placed herself in line to talk to Picasso. She wanted to introduce her parents to Picasso and show them the loom where she had made her scarf.

Winnie brought Mr. Fletcher over to the wall where her drawing of the owl hung.

"Wow, Winnie! This is great! I like how you used light and dark. And there's so much detail," Mr. Fletcher said, way too loudly.

Winnie looked over to see if Picasso had heard him, but she was still busy, talking to a parent near a potter's wheel.

"Look at what you can do in here," Mr. Fletcher exclaimed. He was staring at the supplies on the shelves just as Winnie had when she first visited the hut.

"Isn't it great?" Winnie said. "Come on, the Wileys have already gone outside." Winnie could tell that her father was tired of being rushed, but he didn't complain this time.

They had got in and out of the arts-and-crafts hut without Picasso talking with her father. *Our plan is working beautifully,* Winnie thought as the families wandered over to the dining hall lawn. They were having a barbecue for Visitors' Day and the smell of the barbecue sauce was making Winnie hungry. Now that she was more relaxed, she was ready to eat a mountain of food.

Mr. Fletcher and Winnie got in line and helped themselves to potato salad, corn on the cob, and warm dinner rolls. When they reached the barbecue grills, Winnie looked up and saw Cookie in her no-longer-white apron.

"Fish!" said Cookie. She turned to Mr. Fletcher. "You have quite an artist here."

Mr. Fletcher smiled. "She does love to draw."

"Of course, it must help to have a famous artist for a mother," said Cookie.

"Pardon me?" asked Mr. Fletcher.

Cookie put a slice of chicken on each of their plates.

"Are you Ann Hunt?" Cookie asked the next woman in line.

"No," said the woman with a confused look.

"She isn't here today," said Winnie quickly.

"Oh, that's too bad. You must miss her," Cookie said as she lifted another piece of chicken with her tongs.

Mr. Fletcher's eyelids shut very slowly. His face seemed to be collapsing. Winnie knew that he suddenly understood. "Yes," he said. "We do. We miss her a lot."

Chapter 14

Mr. Fletcher and Winnie ate in silence. They listened to Vanessa and Zoe chatter with their families. Neither one seemed to know what to say. Neither one wanted to say anything in front of anyone else.

Winnie finished her meal and tried munching on the cookies—coconut cookies called macaroons—but they didn't taste sweet.

When the barbecue was coming to an end, the camp director stood up and welcomed everyone. She invited them to participate in camp relays down in the field. Treetops campers and their families would be competing against the slightly older campers in Ledges and their families.

"That's not fair," said Vanessa.

"It's how they do it every year," said Roxie, coming up from behind them. "But just think, next year *we'll* be in Ledges."

The first event was the sack race. Winnie and her father took burlap bags from a pile and stood at the start line with the other campers and their visitors. She looked up at her father's face and could tell that he was distracted.

Mr. Fletcher looked down at her. "It's okay, Win. Let's just have fun now. We'll talk later."

A horn sounded and Winnie and her father took off, hopping in their sacks for the finish line. Winnie fell into a ditch, but Mr. Fletcher kept right on going. The first girl to cross was a Ledges camper: five points for Ledges. Mr. Fletcher crossed second: three points for Treetops.

Winnie and Mr. Fletcher participated in all the events, and for a while, Winnie forgot about Ann Hunt. Together they did the crab walk, the Hula-Hoop pass, and the wheelbarrow race.

Winnie's favorite event was the egg toss. She and her father tossed a raw egg back and forth. Each time one of them caught it, they had to take another step backward. Winnie and her dad did quite well until Winnie tossed the egg a little too hard and hit her dad in the shoulder. Egg dripped down his arm and the front of his shirt. Ledges still remained ahead by three points.

The last event was the three-legged race. The announcer said that pairs needed to be about the same height. Winnie looked at her dad. He towered over her.

"Be my partner?" asked Roxie, coming up beside her.

Winnie looked behind her and saw Roxie's dad tying his leg to Roxie's mom's leg. Nearby, Roxie's stepmother held a new baby. Winnie hadn't noticed the baby before. "Sure," said Winnie.

When the string around their legs was tied tightly, Winnie looked over at her dad to see if he had found a partner. He had. His partner was Picasso.

"Pay attention, Winnie," said Roxie. "The race is about to start."

But it was hard. Her dad and Picasso appeared to have a lot to talk about, and every now and then one of them would burst out laughing. What were they saying? Were they talking about Ann Hunt? Were they making fun of her?

"Ready, set," said the announcer.

BEEP went the horn.

Roxie and Winnie started crossing the field.

Outside legs, inside legs, outside legs, inside legs—the girls had a rhythm. Out of the corner of her eye, Winnie could see that her father and Picasso had tumbled down, laughing.

Winnie sped up. Roxie did, too.

There was all kinds of cheering from the sidelines.

Winnie looked over and saw the determination in Roxie's face. This made her determined too. She and Roxie threw themselves over the finish line.

Chapter 15

Roxie and Winnie came in first place and so did the Treetops girls!

Everyone was hugging and jumping up and down, but Winnie didn't feel like celebrating. She looked back at where her father and Picasso had fallen. They were still sprawled on the ground.

"What's so funny?" said Winnie, walking over and towering above them. They seemed not to notice that the games were over.

"Oh, Fish," said Picasso. "We weren't laughing at your expense."

"What does *that* mean?" said Winnie.

"It means that we weren't laughing at *you*,"

said Mr. Fletcher. "We were having a good laugh over our own clumsiness."

"I better get back to the hut," said Picasso, untying herself from Mr. Fletcher. She stood and brushed grass off her shorts, then she bent down and looked Winnie straight in the eye.

"I want you to know something—Winnie, right? You are one talented girl. Don't you hide that talent behind anything or anyone. Okay?"

Winnie nodded and Picasso walked off.

"See! You told her, didn't you!" Winnie said to her father as they stood alone together in the field.

"I didn't have to," said Mr. Fletcher. "She was so excited to hear that your mother was Ann Hunt, she got on the office computer this morning to do some research. She learned that Ann Hunt is eighty-nine and never had children."

"Really?" Winnie couldn't believe her own foolishness. Of course, anyone would be able to find out all kinds of things about a famous artist. "Was Picasso mad?" she asked.

"Not really," said Mr. Fletcher. "She says that camp is a place where girls often get to be someone new for a while. It's a place where Star can be a star, and she can be Picasso, a famous painter."

Winnie half smiled. So the counselors *did* choose their own names.

"But you should apologize to her."

"I will," said Winnie as they started walking back to where the Wiley van was parked.

"And Dad, I'm sorry that I lied about Mom being alive."

"You must wish it were true," said Mr. Fletcher. "Like me."

"Yeah," said Winnie, trying to put her feelings into words. "But sometimes it's just about feeling unlucky."

"I think everyone feels unlucky now and then," said Mr. Fletcher.

Winnie looked at her dad, who now had dried

egg on his shirt and his left arm. Suddenly she just had to hug him. He was such a good dad.

Mr. Fletcher hugged Winnie back. "So I guess I call you Fish from now on?"

"No! Call me Winnie."

"Really?" said Mr. Fletcher.

"Truly," said Winnie.

"Okay." He started to get in the van, then turned back and winked. "Goodbye, Winnie," he said. "I'll see you next week."

Winnie stood with Vanessa and Zoe and waved goodbye as the cars drove away.

As the girls walked back to Treetops, Winnie spotted Roxie sitting on a large rock at the side of the path.

"Okay if I talk to Roxie?" said Winnie. "I'll catch up with you later."

Winnie left her two friends and walked over to where Roxie was sitting. Water from the lake's edge lapped up against the rock.

"I guess we did it!" said Winnie.

"Yeah," said Roxie, looking up.

Winnie could tell that Roxie didn't feel like celebrating the Treetops victory either. She reached into her pocket and pulled out two of the macaroons she saved from lunch. "Here," she said. "For you."

"Yum," said Roxie. "Thanks."

"What's wrong?" asked Winnie.

Roxie just shrugged.

Winnie hoisted herself onto the rock. "I lied to you," she said.

"What?"

"My mother's not a famous artist."

"What is she?"

"Dead."

"She is?" said Roxie. Winnie could tell that Roxie wanted to ask a million questions, like most kids did when they found out.

"Why did you pretend she was alive?" was the question she chose.

"I'm not sure. It just sort of popped out of my mouth. I think I wanted to see what it would feel like. Then it kept getting more complicated. I'll tell you one thing I know…"

Roxie waited for Winnie to finish.

"I'm done with lying."

Roxie poked a little stick she was holding into the crevice of the rock.

"I lied to you too, you know."

"You did?" asked Winnie. "About what?"

"I didn't tell you that I have a new half sister."

"I never asked you," said Winnie.

"And I didn't answer you when you asked me what was wrong, even though I knew I was feeling sad about everyone else in my family leaving together."

"You were?" asked Winnie.

Roxie nodded. "Now that the baby is here, my father doesn't seem to need me as much."

Winnie placed her hand on Roxie's shoulder and tried to imagine what that would feel like.

She thought about what her dad had said: *Everyone feels unlucky now and then.* She was surprised to realize that this included Roxie too. "Have you told me any other fibs?" asked Winnie. She said "fibs" because she still didn't think that keeping things to oneself was as bad as *lying*.

"Yup."

"What?"

"I hate macaroons," said Roxie.

Both of the girls laughed.

"Let's throw them to the ducks," said Winnie.

They broke the cookies into little pieces and tossed them into the lake. Ducks came paddling over at record speed.

Winnie giggled.

"What?" asked Roxie.

"Floating lunch," said Winnie.

The sky darkened and Roxie and Winnie headed back to their tent. They were partway there when rain burst from the clouds, making the path hard to see.

"Come on!" said Winnie, leading the way.

As they reached the Treetops area, Roxie slowed down and yelled, "Hey, Winnie."

Winnie stopped and turned around.

"We won!" Roxie shouted. "We won the relay competition!"

"We did!" shouted Winnie, holding her arms up high and letting water trickle down her face.

"They're here!" called Vanessa. And with her words, all of the Treetops girls poured out of their tents to join Roxie and Winnie in a crazy dance.

A crazy, lucky, natural-born camper dance in the summer rain.